An Ancient Castle

Robert Graves

AN ANCIENT CASTLE

Illustrated by Elizabeth Graves
With an Afterword by
William David Thomas

Michael Kesend Publishing, Ltd.

First American publication 1981
First paperback edition 1991
© Robert Graves 1980
Afterword © William David Thomas 1980
Illustrations © Elizabeth Graves 1980

Library of Congress Cataloging in Publication Data
Graves, Robert, 1895–
    An ancient castle.
    Summary: When, through the efforts of an
unscrupulous war profiteer, his father is threatened
with dismissal from his job as keeper of an ancient
castle, a young boy helps thwart the conspiracy and
discovers an unexpected treasure.
    [1. Castles—Fiction. 2. Buried treasure—Fiction.
3. Wales—Fiction. 4. Adventure and adventurers—
Fiction.] I. Graves, Elizabeth, ill.
II. Title.
PZ7.G77525An   [Fic]   81–17204
ISBN 0–935576–06–1   AACR2

Contents

CHAPTER ONE

An Ancient Castle

It was nearly three hundred years since anyone had
lived in Lambuck Castle: now none of the rooms had
doors left in the doorways, or windows in the window-
holes, or grates in the fire-places, or floor-boards on the
floors. All the parts of the building that had been made
of wood or plaster had long ago been removed or had
crumbled away: only the stones remained, and not quite
all of those. It was, in fact, only the shell of a castle. But,
like the shell of a boiled egg which someone, after eating
all the inside, has put back upside-down in the egg-cup
for a joke, it looked from a distance as if it was still full
of all the things that one expects to find in a castle –
such as heavy oak furniture, jewels and dresses, well-
stocked store-rooms, soldiers with their armour and
weapons, and horses in stables.

Its shape was square, with four big round towers, one
at each corner, and four more grouped in a square around the main entrance. The walls were over ten feet
thick at the top and twenty feet thick at the bottom and
a hundred feet high. There was a wide path right along
the top of the walls, reached by a steep narrow stone
staircase. If you went inside any of the towers and stood
looking up, there was the sky, shining through; for the
tower-roofs had long ago fallen in. You could tell that

there had once been five rooms in each tower, one on top of the other: for at every twenty feet there came a narrow ledge, running all the way round, made for holding the long wooden floor-beams in place; and there were also window-holes where the windows had been, two to each room, and empty fire-places, one to each room. On a windy day you felt quite giddy, looking up at the sky through the bare walls of a tower, because of the clouds which raced across the round hole at the top. (The same giddy feeling sometimes comes from looking at a tall church steeple, when clouds are moving past – it seems about to fall.) Tufts of grass and fern grew on the narrow floor-ledges and in holes in the wall; and in one of the window-holes near the top there was an elderbush, almost a tree, and an ivy plant in one of the fire-places.

Yes, it was only the shell of a castle, but as strong and safe as ever and well worth refitting with floors and ceilings, doors and windows – though that would have cost a great deal of money; several families could have lived in it comfortably, yet it was not repaired; neither did anyone come to pull it down in order to use the stones for building new houses. Why was this? Partly because it would have seemed a shame to destroy such an old and beautiful building; and partly because the stones were so tightly cemented together that it would have been very difficult indeed to separate them, and they were also much too large and thick to be used for the walls of the cheap sort of houses built nowadays, that are not expected to last many years. Some of the smaller stones had been stolen: from the staircases and the thinner walls of what had been the chapel and the stables. But the chief reason why the castle was not pulled down, and also the reason why it was not rebuilt, was that it belonged to the King of England, one of whose ancestors had built it, six hundred years before, as a fortress for guarding his country against Welsh enemies.

It was one of several huge castles built along the Welsh border: for the Welsh, a poor but fierce race, were fond of making sudden attacks on the nearest parts of England, and carrying off the goods and cattle of the English farmers. When the Welsh ceased to be England's enemies and became allies, these castles were no longer needed as fortresses; and the Kings of England had little use for them. They did not need more than two or three of their many castles and palaces for living in themselves. But on the other hand they did not like selling or giving away anything that they might one day, perhaps, wish to use. So they left their spare castles empty and often forgot even to pay a castle-keeper to look after them.

One knows that when a house or castle is left empty for even a few years, with nobody responsible for taking care of it, the wind and rain soon spoil everything inside; and thieves break in and carry off whatever they find useful – such as doors and grates and window-bars and floor-boards and even stones of convenient size for building. This was what happened to a great many neglected castles in the past; and it had happened here too. But in the reign of Queen Victoria, when most of these castles were more or less in ruins, partly through neglect and partly because they had been knocked about by Oliver Cromwell's cannon two hundred years before, people suddenly began to think of them as old and interesting places. So castle-keepers were paid to look after what was left of them and to watch that they did not tumble down into shapeless heaps of stone.

Queen Victoria's grandson, King George V – or rather one of this King's lords, for a king is too busy to attend to such small matters himself – had chosen Sergeant George Harington as the Castle-keeper of Lambuck Castle. Sergeant Harington was quite a young man at the time but he had lost his right arm in the war against the Germans, so he could do little ordinary work; and this was a suitable occupation for him. The pay was not high but he was allowed to live in what had once been the water-mill which ground corn for the Castle and which was now an ordinary house; and he used to sell picture-postcards of the Castle to the travellers who came to visit it. He also used to tell them true stories about it, if they were interested, and explain how it used to be guarded and point out what rooms had been used for this or that purpose; and they would pay him for his trouble. He had read a number of books of history and knew a great deal about the battles that the Castle soldiers, the English, had fought with the Welsh, and about all the other interesting things that had happened there, especially in the Wars of the Roses and the Civil War. He was so interested in the Castle, indeed, that when a little boy was born to him he was christened Giles in memory of a brave knight called Sir Giles Wyvern, who had been the first Constable of the Lambuck Castle – that is, the captain of the soldiers guarding it.

On each of the Castle turrets – which were small towers built against the side of the big towers and rising a little above the top of the walls – a sentry had once always stood watching the surrounding country for signs of Welsh enemies. The country was fairly flat all around and on fine days the sentries could see for five miles in all directions. If one of them noticed any sign of the Welsh – such as a cloud of dust on the road, or the distant twinkle of light on helmets and spear-points – he would seize the ox-horn which hung on a peg near him and blow a deep, loud note on it. At once all the other soldiers would strap on their armour and seize their bows or spears or other weapons and run into the court-yard in the middle of the Castle to be told by the Constable what to do. If it was not a false alarm, and if the

Constable thought that the Welsh were only a few in number, he would gallop out against them with ten or twenty horse-soldiers, armed with spears and swords, and drive them off. But if the Welsh were coming in great numbers he would tell a few men to guard the gate, and then he would go out with all the rest, not only horse-soldiers but archers and men who fought on foot with long curved knives – perhaps a hundred and fifty soldiers in all – and fight as hard as he could. This was to give time for the English farmers and their families to escape with their cattle and other belongings into the Castle. As soon as they were safely inside, he would lead his army back, fighting all the time, to the Castle, which was protected by a broad, deep moat, full of water. He and his men would cross the drawbridge – a wooden bridge which could be raised and lowered by the men guarding the Castle gateway; and when they were across, up came the drawbridge so that the enemy could not follow except by swimming. Then he would march his men through the gateway, and down would come the heavy portcullis behind them. The portcullis was a very strong gate, made of oak beams, joined criss-cross and faced with iron. It did not open sideways like an ordinary gate but was moved up and down in a slot like a window-frame. Like the drawbridge, it was worked by ropes running on pulleys.

With the portcullis down, everyone in the Castle felt safe; because even if the Welsh swam across the moat – which was impossible for men in heavy armour – they could not force their way through the portcullis, nor could they climb up the smooth, steep Castle walls. They might try with bows and arrows to kill the soldiers standing on the walls or at the windows; but it was much easier for the English to shoot down from the walls than for the Welsh to shoot up at them; and, as for the windows, these were long narrow slits through which one could shoot easily without much danger of being hit oneself. The English not only shot arrows from the walls but threw down great stones to crush the Welsh, and from two small turrets, one on each side of the gateway, poured down kettlefuls of boiling water to scald them to death. There were always large stores of dried meat and corn inside the Castle and barrels of wine and beer, and water in a deep well, and bales of hay for the horses, and a supply of swords and arrows and bowstrings. With these the soldiers could defend the Castle for a very long time without having to surrender. But all this was before the invention of cannon, or rather before the invention of cannon powerful enough to knock holes in such thick stone walls – as they easily can nowadays. Even Oliver Cromwell's cannon, which were not at all powerful compared with modern cannon, did terrible damage to the castles he attacked in his war against Charles I.

Before a battle began, in these days before cannon, the Constable usually sent a messenger on a fast horse to the nearest town to ask for more soldiers to come and drive off the Welsh. But by the time that they arrived, the Welsh had nearly always gone home to Wales with whatever they had managed to steal – horses, sheep, pigs, cattle, carts, sacks of corn, casks of wine, jewels and prisoners. They were not cruel to the prisoners, but fixed a price at which their families in England could buy them back: this was called a ransom. The price was according to the prisoner's importance. If he was a poor farm-servant, the English would have to pay only ten shillings to buy him back; but if he was a knight or a lord, or some relation of a knight or a lord, the ransom they asked might be a hundred pounds or more. In those days everything was very cheap – a sheep cost twopence and a cow two shillings – so that the ransoms were much more valuable than they now seem.

Sergeant Harington used to say that modern war was

a most terrible thing, and that anyone who took pleasure in the thought of modern war was either very stupid or very wicked. It was terrible, he said, because of all the new inventions – aeroplanes that fly high above the clouds and drop bombs on towns to set them on fire; and cannon that shoot enormous shells from twenty miles away big enough to knock down any castle wall; and poison-gas that chokes people to death; and machine-guns, each of which can be managed by a single soldier and shoot six hundred bullets a minute. In the days when the Castle was first built war was more like a game – rather a dangerous game, but not more than rather dangerous. In battles fought then it was rare for more than one or two soldiers to be killed and nine or ten to be wounded; nowadays war is not a game but savage destruction, and a battle is not considered a real battle unless at least a thousand men are killed in it and, say, six thousand wounded. In those days, too, soldiers came close to each other, either on foot or on horseback, and fought hand to hand. But nowadays if an army wishes to capture a village or a hill it is all done by shooting with cannon and machine-guns from a distance and dropping bombs from aeroplanes; and the attacking soldiers hide in deep holes dug in the ground until they think it is safe to go forward, all the enemy being by then either killed or wounded or too shaken and deafened by the noise to fight back. There is seldom any hand-to-hand fighting. Sergeant Harington, for example, had fought in the war against the Germans for three whole years before he lost his arm, and had taken part in several small battles and three big ones, in which thousands of soldiers were killed: yet he had seldom seen any living Germans except far away in the distance, through a telescope, or wounded men, or men holding up their hands to say that they surrendered. He had seen great numbers of dead Germans, of course, killed by cannon and machine-guns and bombs and poison-gas.

The difference between war played as a rather dangerous game, and war carried on as savage destruction, is one of rules, Sergeant Harington used to say. In those old days people did not know so much as they do now and there were far more thieves and robbers and pirates about, and life was much more uncomfortable in every sort of way than it is now. And yet in those old days soldiers – or at any rate the higher sort of soldiers, the knights, who not only rode horses of their own and possessed complete suits of armour, but employed the lower sort of soldiers to fight under them – were most careful about keeping to the rules of war. Just as careful as sportsmen now are about keeping to the rules of football or boxing. The rules of war were known as the 'code of chivalry' – as one talks of the 'code of football' or the 'boxing code'. The lower sort of soldiers fought mostly on foot and wore only a helmet and a breastplate; but to some of them the knights lent horses and proper armour. The knights were their officers and made them behave properly.

The chief rules of the code of chivalry were as follows. Not to strike an enemy from behind when he was not looking; not to aim at the horse on which he was riding, so as to make it fall, but only at the enemy himself; not to use poison; not to hurt women or children or anyone who was not actually fighting; not to kill wounded men or sleeping men or men who had been knocked down and begged for mercy; not to be unkind to prisoners; not to tell lies; not to escape from a battle by throwing away arms and armour. If a knight behaved badly in any of these ways the other knights who heard of it would catch him and break his sword and take away his horse and lop off his spurs and cut his shield in two and call him a renegade and not have anything more to do with him. None of these rules of chivalry are kept in modern war;

which is very curious, Sergeant Harington used to say, when one considers how well modern soldiers usually behave when not actually fighting. And nowadays a man who makes up lies about the enemy to put in the newspapers, or who invents a new poison-gas, or who drops aeroplane-bombs that kill women and children and old men and wounded people and sleeping people is quite likely to be made a knight as a reward, instead of being called a renegade and utterly disgraced.

Sergeant Harington used to say, too, that war is a wicked and horrible thing only when people behave worse in war than they do in peace – 'as happens now,' he added. In the old days men behaved rather better in war than they did in peace, because they were so careful not to break the rules of chivalry and be called renegades; and war was therefore not so bad a thing in its way. But of course even old-fashioned war was very hard on farmers whose horses and cattle and corn were captured by the enemy or who were taken prisoners themselves, and on men who were forced to become soldiers even when they really did not enjoy fighting, and on families who were anxious lest a father or a brother might be wounded or killed.

He was talking one night on this subject in the bar-parlour of an inn near the Castle called The White Lion. Several of his friends were there, including his next-door neighbour, who was a saddler, and the station-master and the village blacksmith – all of whom had been soldiers in the war against the Germans twenty years before. They agreed with what Sergeant Harington said. But a chauffeur, a dark-haired, dark-faced man dressed in a green uniform with silver buttons and called Mr Slark, had drunk too much whisky and began to argue. He said as rudely as he could that Sergeant Harington did not know in the least what he was talking about.

The saddler asked Mr Slark politely whether he had

been a soldier too. Mr Slark said yes, he had been a soldier in that war for four years.

Then the station-master asked him: 'What sort of a soldier?' And Mr Slark answered that he had been in the same regiment as Sergeant Harington and had won a special medal for Distinguished Conduct.

Everyone except Sergeant Harington thought: 'What a brave man!' But Sergeant Harington only laughed. He happened to know that all Mr Slark had done during the war was to drive a General's motor-car. He said: 'I don't call driving a General's car being a soldier. Generals nowadays never go into battles as they did when the Castle was first built; and General's chauffeurs are just like chauffeurs in peace-time. They do not fire guns, drop bombs, or run into any danger whatsoever. And I think it very funny that the medal which the General gave you for being a careful chauffeur was the same sort of medal that soldiers win for doing really brave deeds in battle.'

He should not really have said this, because if Mr Slark had been such a careful driver that the General thought him worthy of a medal, that was to his credit. But Mr Slark had been so rude that Sergeant Harington answered back rather rudely too, without thinking whether what he said was quite fair.

At any rate, his words made Mr Slark very angry. The inn-keeper saw that a quarrel had started and tried to make things right. He said to Sergeant Harington: 'I don't think there is really so much difference between Mr Slark and yourself. You didn't do any real old-fashioned fighting yourself; you were just shot at by cannon and machine-guns and hid in trenches and holes underground and hardly ever saw any Germans except dead ones. You have just told us so yourself!'

Sergeant Harington answered: 'Yes, it wasn't a nice sort of war, I admit. But I was in it, up to the neck, and Mr Slark never even got any mud on his boots.'

Mr Slark could not bear to hear any more. He paid for his whisky and rushed out of The White Lion without another word. A minute later he came back to the door and shook his fist at Sergeant Harington, crying loudly: 'You'll be sorry for this, my friend.' Everyone laughed at him, which made him angrier still. It had been a silly sort of quarrel in which no one behaved very well.

Mr Slark the next day told the person whose chauffeur he was, Sir Anderson Wigg, that Sergeant Harington had used very insulting language at The White Lion. Sir Anderson asked: 'Indeed? And what did he say?'

Mr Slark, who was a bad man, pretended that he did not want to repeat Sergeant Harington's words. At last he said hesitatingly: 'Well, sir, he insulted you. He said that knights nowadays were not a patch on knights in the olden days, and that many men were made knights now for jobs which in the old days would have been too disgraceful for a real knight to do. He mentioned you, sir!'

It was quite untrue that Sergeant Harington had mentioned Sir Anderson Wigg; but it was true enough that Sir Anderson had been made a knight only because during the war against the Germans he had owned a factory which turned out thousands and thousands of tins of jam for the English soldiers. It was not nice jam at all, being mostly made of carrots and swedes with a little bad fruit added; but he put it into brightly coloured tins with his name marked on them – 'Anderson Wigg's Superfine Preserve' – and sold it to the Army for the price of ordinary good jam. He made a very great deal of money out of this fraud, and the soldiers hated the jam when it was served out to them. They used to say that if they ever met Sir Anderson Wigg when the war was over they would have a word or two to say to him. And indeed once or twice it had happened since the war ended that a soldier had met Sir Anderson and kept his promise by saying: 'Oh, so you're Sir Anderson Wigg, are you? What horrible jam you made in the war for us poor soldiers! You ought to be thoroughly ashamed of yourself!' So Sir Anderson began to be a little ashamed but not much. He now said to Mr Slark: 'Thank you, Slark, for repeating this conversation. I shall see that this Castle-keeper is taught a sharp lesson. He has no right to insult me in this way before my servants.'

CHAPTER TWO

A Cruel Plot

We have told a little about the Castle. Now we must tell a little about the village which surrounded it: it had the same name as the Castle – Lambuck – and it was on the main road between the cities of Bristol and Chester. Lambuck was made up of two hundred living houses, twelve shops, a bank, a post-office, a police-station, a temperance hotel, two inns, a school, a railway station and the shed where the fire-engine was kept. There was also a market-hall where the farmers' wives or daughters came on Saturdays to sell their eggs and butter and cheese and fruit and vegetables; and a market-place where, on the first day of every month, the farmers or their sons came to sell cows, sheep, pigs or horses. No factories were near, and there were few excitements except football and cricket matches, and, during the winter, a weekly dance in the market-hall to the music of the village brass band. But sometimes there was a fox-hunt, with men in red coats and women in black habits riding on beautiful horses behind a pack of yelping hounds. The hunts were managed by a man called the Master, helped by a huntsman with a brass horn and another man, with a whip, who kept the hounds from straying. And once a year, in the summer, a Circus came for two or three days to the field near the railway station,

19

and there were roundabouts and coconut-shies and swing-boats. The nearest cinema was ten miles away and a good many people in the village had never been to a cinema in their lives; but were none the worse for this.

Giles had a very happy life at Lambuck. There are always many amusing things to do in the country – even in winter-time when there are no flowers or berries or mushrooms to pick and it is too cold to bathe or even to fish in the streams. He had a few boy-friends of his own age at the village school, but his best friend was a girl, a little younger than himself, called Bronwen. She lived next door to him and was the daughter of the saddler already mentioned. Giles's mother had died soon after he was born, and Sergeant Harington had not married again; so Bronwen's mother used to look after Giles whenever Sergeant Harington was too busy to do so himself; and she mended and washed Giles's clothes and did nearly all the other things that a mother usually does for a child. But she did not give him his meals or bath him, or put him to bed and tell him a goodnight story: that Sergeant Harington liked to do himself, and he did all the cooking too, in spite of having only one hand. So Giles had three homes: the old corn-mill where he lived with his father; and Bronwen's house next door where he went whenever he liked and where he was treated like one of the family; and the Castle where he used to go with his father every day. He had no brothers or sisters.

Sergeant Harington had a room just inside the Castle in what was called the Outer Bailey: this was the part between the main entrance where the portcullis had once slid up and down (but the portcullis had been smashed by Oliver Cromwell's cannon and only the slots were left) and a big inner gate, leading to the Castle court-yard. The gate had been used as a second protection against the Welsh in case they managed to get inside the Castle before the English had time to drop the portcullis. It was not the ancient gate, really, but one that had been put there in Queen Victoria's reign to prevent anybody from getting into the Castle without buying a ticket from the Castle-keeper. Every visitor had to pay sixpence for a ticket, except Giles's boy and girl friends who were let in free by Sergeant Harington on condition that they behaved well. The money from the tickets was partly used for paying the Castle-keeper and partly for repairing dangerous parts of the Castle. The room in the Outer Bailey where Sergeant Harington used to sit and sell entrance-tickets and postcards and guide-books was called the guard-room: it was where once a small guard of soldiers, ready-armed, had always waited to drive anyone away from the Castle who had no business to enter. The room had no ceiling and was very draughty, so Sergeant Harington had built a little wooden hut up against one of the walls, around a fireplace. He put a stove into the fireplace and plastered the walls well to keep out the damp and draughts; and with a table and two chairs and a cupboard and a tiled floor and some pictures it was quite cosy, though rather dark.

One of the two inns in the village has been mentioned – The White Lion; the other was called The Bull. They were both on the same side of the main street. Between them there had once been another inn, the biggest in the village, where in the days before railways all the stage-coaches used to stop to change horses. That middle inn was called The Crown and the station-master used to say that the name 'The Bull' ought really to be changed to 'The Unicorn' to match the Royal Arms of England, which have in them a Crown between a Lion and a Unicorn. Some people thought this very clever: but the inn-keeper of The Bull would not change the name just to please the station-master. It had been called The Bull for two hundred years, he said.

A year before this story begins The Crown had been sold; and everyone had been surprised to hear that it would not remain an inn: it was to be turned into an ordinary living house. The person who bought it was Sir Anderson Wigg. He had never lived in this county before, but he knew that Lambuck was in a fox-hunting district and he wanted to learn to hunt because he thought it rather a grand thing to do. And he had heard that The Crown was going cheap. Soon he changed the name of The Crown to 'Lambuck Hall', to make it seem more important, and rebuilt it in a very elegant style and refurnished it and greatly improved the gardens. But people still called it The Crown, which annoyed him very much.

Nobody really liked Sir Anderson Wigg, who was a bullying sort of man, but he bought plenty of things at the village shops and paid for them, and when he was asked to give money for mending the Church organ, or for the Boy Scouts, or for the Football Club, or for the District Nurse, he always gave the usual amount to show that he was not mean; so the villagers used to touch their caps to him in the street as a sign of respect. The gentry of the neighbourhood, which meant the people who could afford to live in big houses and keep horses for hunting, were quite polite to him too, because they knew that he was very rich and because he was learning to hunt: they thought that if he learned to hunt at his age he must be a good sportsman. There is a hunting code which is kept by all the gentry: it is like the code of chivalry in a way, because if anyone breaks any of the rules the other hunters call him a bad sportsman and have as little to do with him as possible. These are some of the rules. When one is hunting a fox one must not boast, or bully other huntsmen or jostle them and one must not shoot or strike a blow at the fox but must leave the whole business to the pack of hounds themselves and not gallop ahead of them; and one must obey the Master of the pack; and one must not ride over fields where corn is growing; and if anyone falls off his horse in the chase the person riding behind must stop to see if he or she is badly hurt; and if one is a man one must stop to open and shut gates for women riders if the gates are too high to jump over.

Sir Anderson used often to invite the gentry to dinner at his house and give them very expensive food and wine; and as he did not dare to bully them, they thought he was quite a pleasant person. He only bullied his servants and the men and women who worked in his jam factory when he went to see how it was getting on; they did not dare to answer him back for fear of being dismissed. And he bullied his two sons whenever they came home from school for their holidays. He did not allow them to play games with the other boys in the village, because he said that poor children were vulgar. This was not true. Giles and Bronwen were both poor children but neither of them was vulgar; indeed, they had very good manners.

One of the gentry whom he invited several times to dinner, but who was somehow never able to come, was Lord Badger. He was the Lord-Leiutenant of the County. What is a Lord-Lieutenant? Well, in the old days, a Lord-Lieutenant was the general of all the soldiers in a county; but this is no longer so. Nowadays a Lord-Lieutenant is only the head of all the county magistrates. What are magistrates? Well, these are rich men or women who act as judges in not very important cases – such as when small sums of money are stolen or people annoy their neighbours by playing gramophones in the middle of the night or when they break the rules about driving motor-cars. Magistrates are not paid: they do this judging for fun and because they feel that it is useful work that someone else might not do so well as themselves. But really important cases, such as murder and piracy and cheating people out of a great deal of money, are tried by judges who have been properly trained as lawyers: these judges are well paid, because they do not work merely for fun but have to earn their living. The Lord-Lieutenant, besides being the head of all the magistrates in his county, is generally also expected by the King to look after the ruined castles in the county and to see that the caretakers are doing their duty. It was this Lord-Lieutenant, Lord Badger, who, acting for King George V, had chosen Sergeant Harington as Castle-keeper at Lambuck Castle. Lord Badger had been an officer in the same regiment as Sergeant Harington: and had been wounded in the same war and the same battle, in the arm too, but not very badly. He knew that Sergeant Harington was a very honest, careful man: that was how he had come to choose him.

Now, the reason why Lord Badger did not go to dinner with Sir Anderson Wigg was one that few people would have guessed. During the war against the Germans he had held that officers ought not to have an easier life than the ordinary soldiers in the trenches. So, instead of paying for expensive food to be sent him from London, he had always eaten the usual Army food: hard biscuits, and boiled beef in tins, and tea and condensed milk and rum and tinned vegetables – and jam! And like the ordinary soldiers he had hated the jam provided by Sir Anderson Wigg. He knew now that if he went to dinner with Sir Anderson he would have to be polite, and he did not feel that he could easily be polite to a man who had made so much money by cheating poor soldiers who were fighting for their country. For he was not sure yet whether Sir Anderson had changed his habits and become a good sportsman: because once or twice on the hunting field he had seen Sir Anderson do things which were against all the rules. For example he had galloped his horse among the pack of hounds and hurt one of them, and on another occasion he had pretended not to notice that a woman rider had fallen off her horse into a ditch and had rushed on. It might have been carelessness, but it might also have been plain bad manners. So until he was quite sure what sort of a man Sir Anderson now was, Lord Badger, when invited to meals at Lambuck Hall, always made excuses.

But the Deputy Lord-Lieutenant, whom Lord Badger had chosen to do his work for him if he had to be away from the county, went instead of him one day. Sir Anderson was very polite to him and gave him splendid food; and after dinner they sat in the library and talked about the village of Lambuck, smoking cigars and drinking coffee and brandy. Sir Anderson began telling lies about Sergeant Harington, saying that everyone in the village agreed that he was an idle, drunken fellow and ought not to be Castle-keeper. It happened that the Deputy Lord-Lieutenant did not know much about Sergeant Harington, especially about Lord Badger and him having been comrades in the war – and neither did Sir Anderson, or perhaps he would not have dared to tell such wicked lies.

The Deputy Lord-Lieutenant said: 'Thank you, Sir Anderson, for reporting this matter to me. I will make inquiries tomorrow.' For he was stopping that night at Lambuck in Sir Anderson's house, and going home the next afternoon.

When he spoke these words Sir Anderson began to think: 'Now, how can I make it seem that Sergeant Harington is not really fit for his job? For I know that he is really very good at it.'

Mr Slark, the chauffeur, was thinking the same thing. After breakfast the next morning he came to Sir Anderson and said: 'May I suggest, sir, that you ask the

Deputy Lord-Lieutenant to visit the Castle at exactly half past eleven?' For he had been told by the butler, who had overheard the conversation in the Library while he was pouring out the brandy, that the Deputy Lord-Lieutenant was going to make inquiries about the Castle and Sergeant Harington. Sir Anderson asked, 'Why at exactly that time?' Mr Slark grinned and said, 'Because the Castle-keeper won't be there. He is supposed to be at the Castle all the daylight hours, but at half past eleven today he will be at the dentist's. There is a dentist who comes to the village once a week in the morning. I was there myself last week and heard Sergeant Harington arranging to have a tooth pulled out at half past eleven today.'

Sir Anderson thought that this was a good idea, and he and Mr Slark had a private talk about how best to make it seem that Sergeant Harington was unfit to be Castle-keeper. At half past eleven he took the Deputy Lord-Lieutenant to visit the Castle and of course Sergeant Harington was not there. Sir Anderson said: 'People are always complaining that this fellow is absent from his post in the Castle. He is a very drunken fellow. As soon as the public-houses open, he rushes off and sits there drinking all day. Go and fetch him, Slark!'

Mr Slark went off. Then Sir Anderson Wigg said to the Deputy Lord-Lieutenant, 'But this drunken Castle-keeper always has excuses ready for not being at his post. Why, the last time I came here and found him absent he said that he had been at the dentist's. Ha, ha! Not a bad excuse at all! But I expect that this time he will invent a fresh one – unless he is more stupid than I think he is.'

They waited for a while and admired the Castle walls from outside and dropped pebbles into the moat from the fixed wooden bridge that had been put in place of the old drawbridge. After a time the Deputy Lord-Lieutenant asked: 'What other complaints are there against this Castle-keeper?'

Sir Anderson said at once – for Mr Slark and he had arranged this: 'Oh, he allows the Castle to get into a very untidy condition – people throw paper and orange-skins and banana-skins about and he never troubles to pick them up at the end of the day but lets them pile up for many weeks. And he cheats people of pennies and sixpences whenever he gets the chance.'

Then they saw Sergeant Harington coming slowly along with Mr Slark, not walking very steadily, because he had had a bad time at the dentist's. Sergeant Harington suspected nothing and said to the two men: 'Oh, I am sorry I was not here to open the gate. I was at the dentist's.'

Mr Slark gave a wink behind his back, so that the Deputy Lord-Lieutenant, who was easily taken in, believed that Sergeant Harington had really been found drinking at The Bull or The White Lion. He was too polite to say, 'That's a lie, isn't it? You were not at the dentist's, you were at the inn.' And it is a pity that he did not say this, because Sergeant Harington would have made him come along to the dentist's with him to prove that it was no lie. He said nothing, and Sir Anderson smiled to himself, pleased that his trick was working so well.

Then Sir Anderson asked Sergeant Harington: 'We don't have to pay today, do we?'

Sergeant Harington answered: 'Yes, you and your chauffeur must pay sixpence each. But I am told by your chauffeur that this gentleman with you is the Deputy Lord-Lieutenant. If this is so, it means that he has come on behalf of Lord Badger, the Lord-Lieutenant, whom the King has made responsible for the care of this Castle. So he need not pay.'

Sir Anderson gave Sergeant Harington a two-shilling

piece and was given in return two sixpenny tickets and one shilling as change, and then Sergeant Harington opened the gate. He was just about to tell them some interesting story about the Castle, when Sir Anderson exclaimed: 'Where is the other sixpence?'

Sergeant Harington was surprised. He asked: 'Which other sixpence, Sir?'

'I gave you half-a-crown and the two tickets cost one shilling; so you should have given me one shilling and sixpence as my change.'

Sergeant Harington felt in his pocket and pulled out the two-shilling piece. 'This is the coin you gave me,' he said.

'Oh no, it isn't,' cried Sir Anderson. 'Mine was a half-crown with the head of King Edward VII on it. I noticed it particularly.'

Sergeant Harington shouted: 'Are you accusing me of being a thief? You will be the first person who has ever dared to do so. Me a thief, indeed! If the Deputy Lord-Lieutenant would like to search my pockets, he is welcome. He will find no half-crown there.' He was extremely angry, because it is always disgraceful to be accused of being a thief, and it was worse still to be accused in front of the Deputy Lord-Lieutenant. He also remembered how Sir Anderson had cheated him and all the other soldiers over the jam during the war long before, and this made him even angrier.

The Deputy Lord-Lieutenant thought that he was drunk, because of the loud way he shouted and because he had been walking unsteadily when he arrived. He said: 'I don't think that we want such a fuss made about a sixpence do we? There has clearly been a mistake.'

Sergeant Harington said very firmly: 'Not by me, Sir. And if Sir Anderson Wigg thinks that he can get a ticket for nothing by pretending that a two-shilling piece is a half-crown, he is mistaken.'

Meanwhile Mr Slark had slipped through the gate as soon as it was opened and had run across the courtyard to where a large basket was standing full of waste paper and other rubbish. There had been an excursion of school-children to the Castle on the day before and they had thrown sandwich papers and chocolate wrappers and orange-skins everywhere. When they went home, Sergeant Harington had picked up all the rubbish on the sharp point of a stick which he carried for the purpose: he had put the pieces into a satchel and then emptied the satchel into the basket.

Mr Slark deliberately turned the basket upside down and kicked the rubbish about all over the yard. There was a strong wind blowing about the Castle, and it carried the sandwich papers and chocolate wrappers round and round the walls. Then he darted back and slipped through the gate. Sergeant Harington was saying again to the Deputy Lord-Lieutenant: 'I want this matter cleared up, Sir. If you don't believe me about the half-crown, I ask you please to search my pockets.' He did not realize that Mr Slark had been in the courtyard at all.

Sir Anderson said in a nasty voice: 'I don't want to make a fuss about a mere sixpence. I am a rich man. But I don't like to be cheated.'

Sergeant Harington answered: 'And I'm a poor man, but I don't like being cheated any more than you do. Especially I hate being cheated by a rich, mean man.'

Sir Anderson began to use a bullying voice. 'Do you dare accuse me of cheating you? You must be very careful, my man, or you'll be losing your job.'

Sergeant Harington turned white with rage. 'I am not one of your servants or one of the workers in your factory. You cannot take away my job. And what is more, Sir, I have never forgotten the jam that you sold to the Army during the war. It was disgusting jam and I for one would have been ashamed to put my name on a single tin of it.'

Then the Deputy Lord-Lieutenant stepped between them and said to Sergeant Harington: 'You must apologize to Sir Anderson for talking in this way, Castle-keeper.'

Sergeant Harington realized that he had said too much. He answered: 'I will certainly apologize for having mentioned the jam, if Sir Anderson apologizes for having called me a thief.'

Sir Anderson chuckled in a triumphant way and said: 'When you are sober, Sergeant, we can discuss the question of apologies.'

Sergeant Harington did not know what to do. It was no good arguing that he was not drunk; because drunk men always say that they are sober – it is one of the chief signs of drunkenness to think oneself sober. And he could not force the Deputy Lord-Lieutenant to search his pockets. Nor could he prevent Sir Anderson from going into the Castle, now that he had a ticket. He said to himself: 'It will be best to leave things alone now, so as not to let the Deputy Lord-Lieutenant think that I am a quarrelsome person. At any rate, he knows I am not a thief; because I offered to let him search my pockets.'

They went into the courtyard – the Deputy Lord-Lieutenant and Sir Anderson Wigg and Mr Slark and Sergeant Harington. Sir Anderson pointed at the paper flying about and whispered to the Deputy Lord-Lieutenant: 'It is always like this here – rubbish and paper everywhere. Nothing ever gets cleaned up.'

Sergeant Harington was surprised to see such a mess. It had all been quite tidy at twenty-five minutes past eleven when he went to the dentist's. He thought it must have been a sudden whirlwind that scattered the rubbish. He ran to fetch his pointed stick and began picking

up the flying paper.

The Deputy Lord-Lieutenant asked: 'Was there a children's excursion party here this morning?'

Sergeant Harington was too honest to tell a lie. He replied: 'No, Sir, yesterday. I cleaned up all the mess at once, but somehow the basket has been blown over while I was away at the dentist's.'

They then went around the Castle, and into the towers, and up the steep narrow staircase for a walk around the walls to see the view. Then they came down and looked into the Castle-well, the inside of which was green with ferns; and at the ruined chapel where the Castle soldiers used to pray to Saint Hubert, the saint who is said to watch over hunters; and at the large empty store-rooms, and the enormous fire-place in the kitchen over which a spit once used to hang for roasting whole sheep, and at the deep dungeons in which Welsh prisoners were kept. Sergeant Harington also showed the Deputy Lord-Lieutenant a quern that he had found one day when he was cleaning out the moat. It was a round hand-mill, made of two stones placed one above the other, and had been made for grinding corn by hand, if ever the Welsh should capture the proper corn-mill – in the house where Sergeant Harington and Giles now lived – which was worked by the stream that fed the moat.

There had been stone-staircases winding up the turrets to the top, with doors every twenty feet leading into the tower-rooms. But at some time or other the villagers had stolen most of the stones from the staircases – because they were nice flat ones and easy to knock loose and not too big to build houses with. In fact, one could recognize some of them built into the back wall of The Bull. So one could now look up the turrets too, to the sky at the top; and all that was left of those winding staircases were the broken ends of the stairs sticking out of the wall for a few inches here and there. Sergeant Harington said to the Deputy Lord-Lieutenant: 'My boy Giles has climbed up all these turrets except the one yonder, the one next to the West Tower. He is only nine years old but he seems to have no fear. He keeps close to the wall and crawls up from one broken stone to the next. Then he goes out into the tower by the doors and climbs around the narrow ledges where the floors were once laid. He loves this castle. He is now making a model of it in clay with a friend of his, and he says that he must get it exact. So he climbs up into the most dangerous places and takes measurements with a tape measure.'

All that the Deputy Lord-Lieutenant said was: 'Oh, indeed?' But he was thinking: 'I am afraid that I shall have to report to the Lord-Lieutenant, Lord Badger, that this Castle-keeper is drunken, quarrelsome, and a thief and that he allows the Castle to get into a disgraceful mess. It will be bad luck for this boy Giles if his father is turned out of his job; but I'm afraid that I can't help it.'

Then he and Sir Anderson and Mr Slark went off, and Sergeant Harington returned to his room in the Outer Bailey, feeling very disgusted. He was in pain too, because the dentist had pulled out a big tooth at the back of his mouth. But soon Giles came out of school and together they ate bread and cheese and an apple each for lunch; and Sergeant Harington felt happier, because he was very fond of Giles.

CHAPTER THREE

An Interesting Discovery

As they were sitting at lunch Giles said: 'Father, I didn't tell you something last night, because I was keeping it a secret. But I'll tell you now, because you look so sad with your tooth. Well – I climbed up that turret of the West Tower yesterday afternoon when you weren't looking!'

Sergeant Harington exclaimed: 'O Giles, that was very dangerous, wasn't it? You must be more careful. How did you manage to climb up past that place where there are no stones sticking out of the wall?'

Giles answered: 'Well, in Bronwen's garden there is a rope-ladder which her father has fixed to the big pine-tree so that she can climb up to the house I have made for her.'

Sergeant Harington said: 'O yes, the house that you made by nailing boards across two boughs and then roofing it with a piece of packing case covered with old oilcloth. I haven't seen it yet.'

Giles went on: 'I took that rope-ladder with me, and when I came to the difficult part I managed to hook it over a stone far above my head, and climb up. In this way I escaped the difficulty and came to a quite easy piece where the stones stuck out quite far, and climbed to the very top. But that is not all of my story. The most interesting part is that I found that this turret is not quite like the three others. You know that in each of the others there is a little room, leading off the staircase near the top with a stone ceiling and floor?'

Sergeant Harington answered: 'Yes, those are the rooms where the sergeant lived who was in charge of the soldiers in each tower. I went up the East Tower turret once with a ladder and saw what the sergeant's room there was like. It had only a narrow slit-window and was full of sticks from old rooks' nests.'

Giles said: 'Well, the turret of this West Tower has no sergeant's room at all. And the reason why I risked danger in climbing up the stairs was that I wanted to see if there was one. You know that Bronwen helps me with my clay model? Well, in my model I had just put a sergeant's room, with a door, in the turret of the West Tower, just as in the other three corner towers. Bronwen saw it and said: "How do you *know* there's a room there. You haven't been to see." I explained that of course there must be a room there because the West Tower and turret are just the same shape from outside as the others. But she said: "It *may* be so, but you can't say that it *must* be so." Well, she went off to the Castle and came back and said again that there certainly might be a room there, but she was sure that there wasn't a door and she would bet me a penny that there wasn't. And she has won! I am most surprised that she was right, because I don't see why they should have built extra thick walls in that space instead of putting a useful room there; and if there *is* really a room why isn't there a door to it?'

Sergeant Harington asked: 'How on earth did Bronwen guess? You can't see up so far from the bottom of the turret, because of the broken stair-ends getting in the way.'

Giles answered: 'She has just explained to me how she

guessed. It was this: she had noticed that there was no little slit-window looking into the courtyard in the place where the slit-windows of the sergeant's rooms are in each of the other three walls. She said that nobody sensible would block up the only window of a room unless they blocked up the door too.'

'I have never noticed that there is no slit-window there,' cried Sergeant Harington, putting down his glass of beer and jumping up. 'Are you sure that she's right? If she is, I think that you and she have made an important discovery. Let us go and look at once!'

They hurried into the courtyard and looked up at the place, high up, where the slit-window of the sergeant's room ought to have been. Sergeant Harington saw at once that Bronwen was right. There was no slit; but he could see that there had been a slit once, which was now blocked up by stones of a slightly different colour from the rest. Nobody would have noticed this patch, sixty feet above the ground, if he had not been looking very carefully.

That evening, just before he locked up the Castle at dusk, Sergeant Harington borrowed a short ladder and he and Giles carried it up between them to the path around the walls. The path passed by the turret of the West Tower which stood up above it about twenty feet. They also had with them a long rope. Sergeant Harington tied the rope fast to an iron railing which had been fixed beside the path to prevent visitors from falling over the walls if they grew giddy from the height. Then he set the ladder against the side of the turret and climbed up, carrying the loose end of the rope; and then he dropped the rope over the top of the turret and climbed down it. He was soon at the place in the broken staircase which Giles had reached by climbing up from below. Then he took a hammer out of his pocket and began tapping at the wall.

It rang hollow. He called to Giles to hurry up and
fetch a pick-axe. Giles knew where to get one and was
soon back with it. He climbed down the rope himself
and handed his father the pick-axe. Then he balanced
on one of the broken stair-ends and held a pocket-torch
while his father, who had tied the rope around his waist
so as to leave his one arm free, began picking away at
the stones. It took a long time and was very difficult and
rather dangerous work, because if the rope had broken
or come untied Sergeant Harington would have fallen to
his death. But at last he managed to loosen a stone and
wrench it out. It fell with a crash to the bottom of the
turret. Behind it was a dark hole.

Giles said: 'Oh, Father, let me shine my torch in to
see what is there.'

But Sergeant Harington said: 'No, Giles. Before we

look, let us make a hole big enough for one of us to go inside. That will be more exciting.'

In another few minutes he had pulled out several more stones, and there was a hole just big enough for Giles to enter. But in trying to squeeze in, Giles dropped the torch and slipped and almost fell; but saved himself by clutching to his father's leg. It was pitch dark and they had no matches. So they climbed up to the top of the turret again with the help of the rope. When they were safely down again to where the rope was tied to the railing, Sergeant Harington said: 'We'll come back to-morrow: you're trembling with nervousness after your slip. So am I. It would not be safe to explore the turret again this evening. One of us might tumble.'

Giles could hardly sleep that night for excitement and woke very early the next morning. But there was a strong thunderstorm going on, with pouring rain, so they could not do any exploring before breakfast; and after breakfast Giles had to attend school. Then at dinner-time, when the sky was clear again, Sergeant Harington was kept busy showing the Castle to a party of six antiquarians, which means men who are interested in things that have lasted over from ancient times. They asked him so many questions about the Castle that he had no spare time to explore the room. Giles did not want to explore it all by himself, because that would have been unfair to his father. But he climbed down the rope again with the pick-axe and made the hole wider so that a grown person could enter too.

Meanwhile, the Deputy Lord-Lieutenant had gone to call on Lord Badger, the real Lord-Lieutenant, who lived in the town where the cinema was – the same town to which, in the old days, the Constable of Lambuck Castle used to send messages asking for help against the Welsh enemy.

The Deputy said: 'Good morning, Badger. I spent

yesterday at Lambuck staying with Sir Anderson Wigg. He was complaining about the Castle-keeper there. Do you happen to know the fellow?'

Lord Badger answered: 'Yes, I do know him, I know him very well. His name is Harington and I chose him myself. What complaints against him can Sir Anderson possibly have made?'

The Deputy answered: 'That he is never on duty, that he is often drunk, that he allows the Castle to get dirty and that he steals money from the visitors.'

Lord Badger said: 'These are very serious charges. Has Sir Anderson put them in writing? I hope he has, because I am sure that they are all lies, and, as you know, if anyone makes an accusation which is a lie and writes it down it is called "publishing a libel", and the person accused can go to a lawyer and the lawyer will make a complaint to the judge and in the end the accuser will have to pay a great deal of money to the person accused.'

The Deputy answered: 'No, Sir Anderson did not write anything down. And I am much afraid that the accusations are true. I went to the Castle at half past eleven, and Sergeant Harington was not there as it was his duty to be. He was drinking at an inn and had to be fetched from there. And then he pretended that he had just been to the dentist.'

Lord Badger interrupted: 'Did you yourself find him at the inn? How do you know that he wasn't at the dentist's?'

The Deputy had to admit that he only thought he had been at the inn. But he added that Sergeant Harington certainly was walking in rather a wobbly way and seemed confused.

Lord Badger asked: 'Have you ever had a tooth pulled out, with gas? Did you feel perfectly steady and clear-minded immediately after?'

Then he went across to the telephone and asked for no. 3715. That was the telephone number of the town dentist who went by train to Lambuck once a week to attend to people there who could not manage to come to town. He asked: 'Is that Mr Ossilage? This is Lord Badger speaking. Could you tell me, please, what patient you were attending at 11.30 yesterday.'

Mr Ossilage answered: 'One moment, I must look at my engagement book, your Lordship.' Then he found the page in the book and said: 'Yes of course. I was pulling out an upper molar on the right jaw of a Mr Harington. It was a difficult job and my assistant had to give him gas.'

'Thank you,' said Lord Badger. 'That is all I wanted to know.' Then he turned to the Deputy and repeated Mr Ossilage's words. The Deputy looked very foolish.

Lord Badger said: 'We now know that Sergeant Harington wasn't drunk, and that he had a perfect right to be absent from his duty on that occasion; because it was the only time that he could go to the dentist without coming all the way here to town and being away for a whole morning. Now, tell me about the other accusations. Let me hear this cock-and-bull story about Sergeant Harington being a thief. He is one of the most honest men I have ever met.'

The Deputy told him about the sixpence. Lord Badger said, rather sternly: 'I am sorry that you did not search him, as he asked, instead of believing Sir Anderson's story. You would certainly not have found the half-crown – be sure of that! Either it was a stupid mistake on Sir Anderson's part or else he was trying to cheat Sergeant Harington. I think that Sir Anderson owes him an apology.'

'Well, at any rate,' said the Deputy, 'Sergeant Harington was very rude to Sir Anderson.'

'Yes,' said Lord Badger, 'and if I had just had a tooth

pulled out with gas and if Sir Anderson Wigg, of all men, called me a thief, so should I have been rude – much ruder, probably.'

The Deputy then said: 'Anyhow, the Castle was in a terrible mess.' He told the story about the flying paper, and about Sergeant Harington having admitted that the children's excursion had taken place the day before.

Lord Badger thought for a moment. Then he asked: 'Did you go into the towers and turrets afterwards?'

'Yes,' replied the Deputy.

'And was there any paper or other rubbish lying about in them?'

'No,' said the Deputy. 'The mess was only in the courtyard.'

'Then,' said Lord Badger, 'you can be sure that Sergeant Harington was telling the truth. The children would have scattered the paper and orange-peel in the towers and turrets as well as in the courtyard. I am sure that when you were not looking the chauffeur went and upset the rubbish basket and kicked the rubbish about on purpose. The wind scattered the papers about the court, but they did not get inside the towers.'

The Deputy said: 'My goodness, Badger, I believe that you're right. I remember a bit of banana-skin sticking on the chauffeur's right boot and wondering how it got there.'

Then Lord Badger said: 'I am going to Lambuck this very afternoon to clear up this whole matter. I *won't* have Sergeant Harington accused falsely like this.'

'I am very sorry,' said the Deputy. 'I was quite taken in. Sir Anderson Wigg gave me a very good time at his house, so naturally I believed him.'

Now the reason why Lord Badger had appointed a Deputy Lord-Lieutenant to do his work for him was that he was soon going for a three months' holiday to Africa to see lions and elephants and giraffes running wild. One

day he had come to Lambuck to see the Circus with his grandchildren. He had watched the sad-looking mangy lions, in a cage at the Circus, jumping through paper-hoops while their trainer cracked his whip at them. And he had watched the old elephant, with sawn-off yellow stumps instead of tusks, doing rather silly tricks for its driver: such as drinking a bottle of beer, and banging a drum with a drumstick held in its trunk, and walking on its hind legs. He had suddenly said to himself: 'I should like to see a really wild elephant crashing through the jungle – a strong young elephant with long white, sharp tusks. And I should like to see a tall giraffe galloping like mad across the plain, and great herds of striped zebra coming down to drink at a lake. And I should like to watch a fight between brave negroes, armed with spears and shields, and a really fierce lion.

I must go to Africa as soon as possible. I shall appoint a Deputy Lord-Lieutenant to do my work while I am away.'

It was now only two days before his ship sailed for Africa, so he had little time to spare. He went to the telephone again, the Deputy still being in the room, and asked: 'Give me Lambuck 48, please.'

Soon someone said: 'You're through' and someone else said: 'Hullo, this is Lambuck Hall.' It was Mr Slark, answering the telephone at Sir Anderson Wigg's house.

Lord Badger said: 'This is the Lord-Lieutenant of the County speaking. Is Sir Anderson Wigg at home?'

Mr Slark answered: 'Hold on a minute, your Lordship,' and ran to tell Sir Anderson.

Sir Anderson whispered to Mr Slark: 'Excellent. The Deputy Lord-Lieutenant has reported the Castle-keeper.

Now, let's see what happens.' And he rubbed his hands together in a vulgar way to show that he was pleased.

Lord Badger told Sir Anderson Wigg over the telephone that he had heard that there had been trouble that morning at the Castle. He said: 'I am most vexed that this trouble should have occurred. Will it be convenient if I come tomorrow afternoon at four o'clock to make an enquiry on the spot? Will you be there to meet me? I am not going to allow this sort of thing to happen again.'

Sir Anderson naturally thought that Lord Badger intended to come and dismiss Sergeant Harington. He said: 'I shall be delighted to meet you at four o'clock. Or will your Lordship do me the honour of coming to luncheon at my house beforehand?'

Lord Badger replied: 'No, thank you, Sir Anderson, I am too busy. I sail for Africa two days hence and still have a lot to do. Every moment is precious. Goodbye until tomorrow.' This was true, but in any case he would have refused the invitation. He did not wish to accept any favours from Sir Anderson, because then it would be more difficult to speak sternly to him if he found that the accusations against Sergeant Harington were all lies.

The Deputy said that he would come too, if Lord Badger wished. 'Certainly I wish you to come,' said Lord Badger. 'I want you to help me.'

CHAPTER FOUR

A Sensible Lord-Lieutenant

The next day, it will be remembered, was the day that there was the thunderstorm before breakfast and that Sergeant Harington and Giles were kept waiting for a chance to go into the hole that they had made in the turret-wall of the West Tower. Giles came out of after-noon-school at exactly four o'clock; and he and Bronwen, whom he had told about the hole, because he had no secrets from her, ran along to the Castle at once. They arrived just as a big blue car drove up. Out stepped Lord Badger and the Deputy and a little man with glasses who was Lord Badger's secretary. Lord Badger, it should have already been said, was tall and rather thin with white moustaches and bright blue eyes. He wore a tweed suit and carried a cane with an amber knob on the top.

Sir Anderson Wigg was waiting on the wooden bridge to meet him, with Mr Slark standing behind. Mr Slark was carrying his master's mackintosh over his arm. Sir Anderson, who, it should have already been said, was a chubby man with a red face and nearly always wore black clothes as if he were living in London, not in the distant country, came running up and shook hands. He said to Lord Badger: 'It is very good of your Lordship to come down to see to this little matter for me when you are so busy.'

Lord Badger answered: 'Humph' which meant: 'Perhaps I have other reasons for coming than just doing you a favour, Sir Anderson Wigg.'

Giles ran into the Castle to warn Sergeant Harington that Lord Badger was coming. He knew Lord Badger by sight because, besides being the Lord-Lieutenant, he was also the Master of the Fox Hounds that, as has been said, used sometimes to come hunting at Lambuck. Giles found his father still telling the party of antiquarians stories from the history of the Castle. Ordinary people think that in half an hour they can see everything worth seeing in a castle; but antiquarians can spend days there and still be interested. These antiquarians had been in the Castle now for more than four hours. Sergeant Harington was telling them the sad story of the Constable of the Castle whose name Giles had been given – Sir Giles Wyvern.

This was the story. Sir Giles had defended the Castle bravely against a large Welsh army, but in a fierce battle outside the gates most of his soldiers had been killed. When he rode back over the drawbridge and through the gateway and the portcullis came slamming down behind him, he only had about twenty soldiers left of whom six were wounded. They were all bold men and with their help he could have managed to defend the Castle easily, if there had not been a traitor, one of the Castle cooks, who secretly poisoned the water in the well so that two wounded soldiers who drank of it died instantly. The same traitor pulled the stoppers out of the casks in the cellar where the beer was kept. There was nothing left to drink but one barrel of wine, which Sir Giles kept in his own room, and a cauldron of water in his private kitchen. The wine and water would only last for ten days. He feared that then either everyone would die of thirst, because it was summer and there was no sign of rain; or else he would be forced to surrender the Castle to the Welsh in exchange for water. As for the water in the moat, the Welsh shouted to the English: 'We advise you not to let down buckets from the walls into the moat. We have poisoned the water there too.'

Two days later Sir Giles' wife, the Lady Eleanor, was shot by an arrow by a clever archer as she was peeping through a slit-window, and died at once. Sir Giles, mad with rage and grief, ordered the portcullis to be raised and the drawbridge lowered, and galloped out to take vengeance. He killed two Welsh knights and several Welsh foot-soldiers, but it was a hopeless fight and he was stabbed to death at last. The guard at the gate quickly shut themselves in again by raising the draw-bridge and lowering the portcullis, and then began shooting arrows at the Welsh as they tried to cross the moat on rough rafts, and throwing down boiling water at them − for the poisonous well-water was still useful for this purpose. They cried: 'Sir Giles is dead but we shall never surrender.'

That night there came a fierce thunderstorm. The soldiers in the Castle caught the rain in a huge piece of canvas stretched on the ground, with the corners pulled up so that it made a sort of bath. Then they poured the water from this bath into the empty beer-barrels and had enough to last them for some weeks. So the Welsh did not win the Castle after all, and a month later a big English army came from Chester and drove the Welsh off.

This was the story that Sergeant Harington was telling to the antiquarians: who were standing in the very cellar where the treacherous cook had let all the beer out of the barrels. Giles knew the story well, but he politely waited while his father told the last sentence about the English army coming to the rescue along the road from Chester. Then he said: 'Hurry, Father, Lord Badger is here.'

Meanwhile Sir Anderson was talking to Lord Badger about fox-hunting, and Lord Badger was saying 'yes' and 'no' but not much else. He was busy watching Mr Slark out of the corner of his eye, because he remembered about the banana-skin on Mr Slark's boot.

When Sergeant Harington came running up, Lord Badger, to Sir Anderson's surprise, shook him by the hand and said: 'Well, Sergeant, I am glad to see you again. What a long time since we last met! I am always too busy with my hounds, when I come hunting here, to visit you at the Castle. I looked out for you that day when I brought my grandchildren here to the Circus, but you were nowhere about.'

Sergeant Harington smiled and answered: 'No, Colonel' – he still called Lord Badger 'Colonel' because he had been his colonel during the war against the Germans – 'I couldn't get away that day. I was on duty here showing visitors round, as usual.'

Lord Badger said: 'Of course; you were always a man who could be trusted to do what was expected of you! Is this your little boy? How he has grown!' He patted Giles on the head.

Sir Anderson began to feel uncomfortable. Things were not going as he would have liked. He said: 'But Lord Badger, this man was insufferably rude to me yesterday!'

Lord Badger answered politely: 'So the Deputy Lord-Lieutenant has told me. But I understand that Sergeant Harington offered to apologize for his rudeness if you would apologize for accusing him of stealing sixpence. And since you did not apologize, neither did he.'

Mr Slark then sneaked into the Castle courtyard through the gate, thinking that nobody would notice him. He had been careful to buy his ticket before Lord Badger arrived. When he bought it, Sergeant Harington had said to him: 'Mr Slark, I have been thinking things over, and I know now that it was very wrong of me to say what I did about the medal you won for Distinguished Conduct. You did your duty and evidently you did it well; and if I was in the trenches being shot at by the Germans while you were driving the General's car, out of danger, well, that was just my bad luck. Will you forgive me and shake hands?' But Mr Slark had just sneered and answered: 'Shake hands? Not me! You ask me to shake hands only because you are afraid what my master, Sir Anderson Wigg, is going to do to you. You think I will perhaps ask him to let you off. But it's too late now.'

When Mr Slark came sneaking back, half a minute later, Lord Badger smiled to himself. He felt sure that Mr Slark had been hiding a bag of rubbish under his mackintosh and scattering it around the courtyard to make it seem as though Sergeant Harington had again left the Castle in an untidy state. He said to Sir Anderson: 'We will discuss the matter of the rudeness more fully in a few minutes. Meanwhile I want to look round the Castle to see how well Sergeant Harington keeps it.'

As soon as they came into the courtyard, there were dozens of pieces of paper lying about. Lord Badger said to Sergeant Harington: 'Hullo, what's all this?'

Sergeant Harington's face turned very grave. He said: 'This rubbish was not here a moment ago. You can ask the six gentlemen I have been talking to. They are antiquarians and have been here ever since the dinner-hour.'

Lord Badger answered: 'I will not trouble you to do that. You know that I can trust your word, Sergeant.' Then he told Giles: 'My boy, will you please collect a few of those pieces of paper for me?'

Giles ran off and collected several large sheets of crumpled newspaper. But Bronwen, who was a clever little girl, understood what Lord Badger meant. She collected

the smaller, more interesting bits of paper. Among these
were: a letter written on a rough piece of note-paper;
some thin pieces of paper like those used for wrapping
up oranges; and a torn bill from the Lambuck coal-
merchant. She brought them to Lord Badger who said:
'Thank you, my dear, these are just what I want.'

First he looked at the coal-bill, and next he read the
letter. Lastly he examined two pieces of the wrapping
paper and handed them to the Deputy. 'What do you
make of this paper?' he asked. The Deputy who, as will
have been guessed, had not a very sharp eye, looked
again and said: 'These are orange wrappings. I suppose
that children have come here and eaten oranges and
carelessly thrown away the paper – or so it seems at first
sight,' he added, so that Lord Badger should not think
him stupid if this was a mistake.

'Yes,' said Lord Badger. 'It does look like that at first sight. But if you read the name printed on them you will see that they are grapefruit wrappings. Children do not suck grapefruit like oranges. Grapefruit are too big and juicy and clumsy for sucking, and also very expensive. One cuts them in two and puts the halves on a plate and eats the inside with a silver grapefruit spoon. But if some very greedy, very rich children did eat them here, what has happened to the skins? I suppose you will say that the little beggars ate them, skins and all?'

Then he handed the Deputy the torn bill from the coal-merchant and said: 'Will you read this out, please?'

The Deputy read out: 'To supplying two tons of best kitchen coal, and four hundredweight of coke, £4.3.6. To Sir Anderson Wigg, Lambuck Hall. Sept. 30th.'

Sir Anderson's red face grew redder still. He said: 'How extraordinary! I don't know how the coal-merchant's bill got into the Castle. He must have dropped it here himself on the way to my house.'

Lord Badger asked Sergeant Harington: 'Was the coal-merchant here today, or perhaps one of his assistants?'

Sergeant Harington answered: 'No, Colonel. And no rich greedy children either.'

'I thought not,' said Lord Badger in a dry voice. 'The bill is more than a week old, and the coal-merchant would not have brought such an old bill along. And it was obviously dropped here since breakfast-time today, because it is quite dry. If it had been dropped yesterday, or the day before, or early this morning, it would be wet through – and so would all this other paper.'

Lord Badger was not a particularly clever man, but he had taught himself to notice small things; because when one is a magistrate and has to judge people, accused of crimes, who say that they are innocent, often it is difficult to know whether they or their accusers are telling the truth. Often a very small thing that most people would not notice will show a careful magistrate that someone is telling lies – sometimes the accuser and sometimes the accused and sometimes both at once. This time it was easy for him to guess that Sergeant Harington was being unjustly accused; because good people seldom change much, and he remembered what Sergeant Harington had been like when he was a soldier. He had been a truthful man and also very tidy and not a drunkard; in fact his one fault was saying very rude, angry things if he was provoked, without caring whether the person who provoked him was rich or poor, important or unimportant.

There remained the letter, which was written with an indelible pencil in a very clumsy handwriting. Lord Badger said loudly, so that everyone present could hear: 'Since the person to whom this letter is written is not mentioned by name, and since the person who has written it only signs himself "An Old Soldier", I think that it is not too private to be read aloud. I shall have the pleasure of reading it aloud myself.'

Then he read from the letter as follows:

Potford, Cheshire. Oct. 17

Sir,

I understand as you are now living at Lambuck a few miles off of Potford where I live, and as you as turned the old Crown into a fine house for yourself. Well, Sir, I as always wanted to know where you was a-living, so as I could keep a promise I made myself twenty-three years ago when I was a youngster in the Army. I promised myself then as I would say a word or two to you on a certain subjeck. Yes and I would come along now and do so, only I am a cripple from the war and cant leave my bed, so this ere letter must do instead. Well, Sir, I think it a wicked shame as a gentleman like you should ave made such a pile of money by selling rotten jam to the Army in such pretty-looking tins too. It was the very rottenest jam as I or my mates ever tasted in our born lives and it would be very interesting to no what on earth it was as you put into your jam to make it taste so very nasty. But I suppose as that must remain your own trade secret and you will carry it with you to your grave. Goodby now, Sir, and I hope as you may long remember my words, which is: 'my greatest ope is that one day by mistake you may eat a mouthful of your own terrible jam, and I ope as it chokes you and serve you well right.' Yours truly,

An Old Soldier.

Lord Badger looked very keenly at Sir Anderson, who was opening and shutting his mouth in confusion. After a long silence he said: 'Sir Anderson, I do not know to whom this letter was addressed. But I can guess. For I can well remember the jam to which the writer refers. And (speaking as an ordinary private person, not as a public official) I must say that the sense of the letter seems to me far better than the spelling. I can also guess who scattered all this litter here – I mean this chauffeur of yours.' Here Lord Badger looked sternly at Mr Slark. 'Will you please tell him to lay down on the ground everything that he is now holding over his arm.'

But Sir Anderson still could only open and shut his mouth; so Sergeant Harington went quickly over to Mr Slark and took the mackintosh from him. Hidden under the mackintosh was a large string bag, and when Lord Badger looked at it, he found that it still had a few scraps of waste paper in it. One of them was the envelope in which the Old Soldier's letter had come (the writing was the same) and it was addressed to Sir Anderson Wigg, 'The Crown', Lambuck. It was clear to everyone that Mr Slark had been stupid enough to get the waste paper from Sir Anderson's own waste-paper basket.

Then Lord Badger said: 'Sir Anderson, your chauffeur will be charged with wilfully scattering waste paper on Crown property. I hope that the magistrate in front of whom he is brought will not let him off lightly. But that is not all. It remains for Sergeant Harington to decide whether to accuse your chauffeur and yourself of conspiracy. Under the laws of this country, two or more people who make a plot to cheat anyone out of money or employment are guilty of conspiracy and can be sent to prison for a long time. If Sergeant Harington makes this accusation, my Deputy will be there in Court and will tell the Judge exactly what happened yesterday. And the Judge will perhaps decide that it was not just an accident that my Deputy was led to believe, by what was said and done by yourself and your chauffeur, that Sergeant Harington was not doing his duty. What I mean is this: the Judge may decide that it was a plot all arranged beforehand between you two, and that the same trick was tried again today.'

Sir Anderson Wigg was really frightened now. It was quite true that he and Mr Slark had plotted together, and if he denied this to the Judge, the Judge might not believe him – especially if Mr Slark confessed at once that he was guilty, in order to be given a smaller punishment than he deserved.

At last he said: 'Will the Castle-keeper accept a full apology from me and forgive me? I will explain why I did what I have done. It was because I was told that Sergeant Harington had said one night in The White Lion that I was a cheat, and that I should never have been made a knight.'

Sergeant Harington cried: 'I never said anything of the sort! I expect it was Mr Slark who told you that.'

'Yes,' answered Sir Anderson, 'it was Slark, and I am sorry now that I believed him.'

Lord Badger said: 'What I cannot understand, Sir Anderson, is why, just because you were told that someone had called you a cheat and unworthy to be a knight, you should have done everything possible to prove that he was right.'

There was a long silence after this.

At last Sergeant Harington said: 'I accept your apology, Sir Anderson, and I will not bring any charge of conspiracy against you and Mr Slark. I consider myself lucky that things have not turned out any worse for me. It all started by my getting angry with Mr Slark, when he said that I was talking nonsense about modern war, and sneering at the medal he had won. This will be a lesson to me. But I am not going to tell Mr Slark that I am sorry, because when I told him so, half an hour ago, he refused to shake hands.'

Sir Anderson thanked Sergeant Harington for being so generous, and also thanked Lord Badger for being so fair, and then he went slowly away, with Mr Slark trailing behind him. They both looked most ashamed of themselves.

CHAPTER FIVE

A Fortunate Ending

When they had gone out through the gate, Lord Badger exclaimed 'Pah' as if he had a bad taste in his mouth. And then, looking at his gold watch, he said: 'I suppose that I had better be going home. Everything seems settled.'

Sergeant Harington said: 'Colonel, before you go, would you like to explore a room in the Castle where I think that nobody has been for hundreds of years?'

Lord Badger grew very excited at these words, and so did the six antiquarians who had gathered around to listen to what was being said. He answered: 'Certainly, Sergeant, lead the way! There is nothing that would please me better.'

'It means a bit of climbing, I am afraid,' said Sergeant Harington. 'The room is more than half-way up that turret over there.'

'Then I'll send for the Fire Brigade and get them to bring ladders. I am the head of all the Fire Brigades in the county.'

Giles ran off and called the Fire Brigade. He had the fun of riding on the fire-engine, a thing which he had always longed to do. The head of the Fire Brigade drove the fire-engine along at a rush, blowing his klaxon-horn loudly, thinking that the Castle was on fire. He forgot that it was only the shell of a castle, with nothing in it that could burn except Sergeant Harington's little hut. Giles had tried to explain to him that there was no fire, but he had been too busy to listen.

Tied to the engine was a long ladder, in pieces that could be joined together, and when the Fire Brigade arrived Lord Badger told the head to set this ladder up inside the turret. It was a long time before he could make the head understand that it was not necessary to pump water from the moat through the hose; because there was no fire in the Castle to put out.

'It would be a little difficult to set the Castle on fire, you will agree,' he said. 'So be sensible, please. Leave those hosepipes alone and put your ladder up in the turret of the West Tower, as I have asked you to do three times now.'

When this had been done, Lord Badger said: 'Now, Sergeant, since you found this room, you will have the honour of going in first.'

But Sergeant Harington answered: 'No, Colonel. To be honest, my boy Giles really found it. Let him have the honour of going in first.'

But Giles said: 'No, Father, Bronwen really found it. It was all her idea that I should look for it.'

So they all went up the ladder in this order: first Bronwen, then Giles, then Sergeant Harington, then the Lord-Lieutenant, then the Deputy Lord-Lieutenant, then the six antiquarians. Only the secretary with the glasses stayed behind. He said that he was afraid of climbing up ladders.

When they reached the hole, Giles handed Bronwen his pocket torch and she went in, with Giles just behind her. Then they flashed the torch around and both shouted 'Oo, look! Hurrah!'

Sergeant Harington came in next and when he looked he cried: 'My goodness!' And Lord Badger exclaimed:

'Well, upon my word!' And so did the Deputy. As for
the six antiquarians, they began shouting and jabbering
at each other like a cageful of monkeys.

Indeed, it was a very remarkable sight. They were
standing in a room with a sand-covered floor and white-
washed walls and ceiling. It was about twenty feet long
and twenty feet wide, and not very stuffy because it had
had time to air since the hole was made the evening
before. It was full of interesting things. There was a big
wooden bed; and three wooden chests and a heavy table
with two tall bronze candlesticks on it; and a huge wood-
en chair, like a throne; and two complete suits of armour
standing in a corner, and a stack of weapons, and some
jugs and basins in one corner and a great many smaller
bundles and boxes arranged about the place. There had
evidently been still another chest there once, because
they noticed a pile of rotten wood near the bed among
which shone gold and silver coins. Oak, of which the
bed and two of the other chests were made, lasts for a
very long time; this must have been made of pine or
some other soft wood and it had crumbled away. Lord
Badger opened the chests and found in one of them,
which was made of cedar, not oak, what had once been
a pile of rich silk and woollen dresses, but there was not
much left of them except bits of gold and silver embroid-
ery – moths had eaten the rest; and in one of the oak
chests he found a pile of books, some written in Latin,
which was the language they spoke in church when the
Castle was first built, and some in Norman-French,
which was the language which the knights spoke. They
were not printed, but written very neatly by hand with
beautiful little pictures to make them more interesting.
In the remaining chest were five heavy gold chains; six
gold rings, one of them with an amethyst in it; six silver
cups; six drinking horns, three of them with silver rims,
and three with gold rims; a dagger in a jewelled scabbard

– but the blade was all rust; an olive-wood box, with golden hinges, full of cockle-shells which some pilgrim had brought home, as good-luck charms, from the Holy Land; the tooth of a walrus; a carved ivory statue of Saint Hubert; and several other curiosities.

The antiquarians nearly went mad with excitement. Everything, they kept saying, was in a wonderful state of preservation – because the door and window having been carefully blocked up and the floor and ceiling being made of stone and the walls well plastered, the rain and damp had never got in to spoil things. They all agreed that this was the first time a furnished room had ever been discovered in England exactly as it had been left six hundred years before. They said that the books alone were worth thousands of pounds, and that the armour was worth a huge sum too, because it was very beautiful armour, inlaid with gold, and the only really complete set of knight's armour of that period that still existed. There was a painted shield with it, and one of the antiquarians recognized the pattern on it as the arms always worn by the men of the Wyvern family on their shields, and on their surcoats (which were light riding-coats) and on the saddle-cloths of their horses.

One said one thing and one said another, arguing as to how long ago these things had been put here and the room sealed up. But Lord Badger settled the argument. He asked them to look at the coins, and none of them were found to be later in date than the year when Sir Giles Wyvern died. So it seemed certain that it was he who had sealed up the room. Some of the coins were very rare ones for which coin collectors would willingly have paid a hundred pounds each. The antiquarians then said that Sir Giles must have hidden all the treasure here at the time when he expected the Castle to be captured by the Welsh. He must have asked one of his soldiers to build up the doorway of the room secretly

with stones and block up the window so that the Welsh should not suspect that there was a room there at all. No doubt he hoped that one day the English would win the Castle back and then, if he were still alive and free, he would find his treasures safe and sound. Perhaps the man who helped him was one of the wounded soldiers who was poisoned, so that when Lady Eleanor and Sir Giles were both killed, nobody was left alive who knew the secret; and since the upper rooms of the West Tower were only used as store-rooms nobody noticed that the sergeant's room was blocked up.

Lord Badger said to Sergeant Harington: 'You will be a very rich man before long. I suppose that you will not want to remain here as Castle-keeper.'

Sergeant Harington asked: 'What do you mean? This treasure doesn't belong to me. It belongs to the King.'

'Yes,' said Lord Badger, 'but it is what they call Treasure Trove. According to the laws of England, if someone finds treasure that has been hidden long ago and forgotten, it becomes the property of the King. But the King gives the finder four-fifths of the value of what has been found, and sends the treasure to a museum where everyone can look at it.'

Sergeant Harington said: 'Well, that is good news! I shall be very glad of the money. But it would be a great pity to send this treasure to a museum. It ought to stay here in this room for visitors to see it. This room itself ought to be made into a museum, with a new staircase built up the turret to it. And I should like to remain here as Castle-keeper, if I may.'

Lord Badger said: 'Of course you may. And I quite agree about making this room into a museum. I shall write to the King at once and suggest it. Yes, this turret staircase ought to be rebuilt and the slit-window opened, and everything left just as it is now – except that the smaller valuables ought to be taken out of the chests and off the floor and put in glass cases where people can see them better and not spoil them by touching.'

Later Lord Badger repeated his plans to his secretary and said: 'Make a note of that please, Mr Hunter, and let me have the letter to sign and seal this evening.'

For the secretary, who looked a most useless sort of man, was really of great help to Lord Badger. Lord Badger usually knew what to say when any difficulty arose, but seldom knew how to put it down in what is called 'proper official form' – which means the old-fashioned complicated way in which letters are written to the King by any of the King's lords, ministers or servants or by one lord, minister or servant to another. The secretary, on the other hand, seldom knew what to say when a difficulty arose, but could always put down in proper official form whatever Lord Badger said. 'The more important the lord,' the secretary used to say, 'the more old-fashioned and complicated the official form must be when he writes letters to the King or to other lords.' Lord Badger was 'Hereditary Warden of the Marches', which meant that his ancestors had always protected the English frontier against the Welsh, and he was a very important lord indeed. So the secretary had a very complicated letter indeed to write for Lord Badger to sign. Instead of beginning:

> Your Majesty,
>   I am writing to ask you to do me a favour, if you please: it is about Lambuck Castle.

the letter went like this:

> Right puissant Liege Lord,
>   Let Me Entreat and Beseech of your Grace to Confer and Convey upon Me a Boon which these Presents Clarigate: as touching your Stronghold and Donjon of Saint Hubert in the Hundred of Llanbach, vulgarly named Lambuck. . . .

When the secretary had asked Lord Badger a few questions about what sort of glass cases he wanted, and so on, in order to make no mistakes in the letter, Lord Badger turned to Sergeant Harington and said to his great surprise: 'Meanwhile, Sergeant, for the sake of old times, would you like to come to Africa with me for a short holiday and see wild animals running about free in their native habitat? One of my party has just broken his leg and cannot go: it is the chance of a lifetime for you!'

Sergeant Harington thanked him but asked: 'What about my boy Giles? I can't leave him behind. And what about the Castle?'

'Oh, the Castle will be all right. I can find someone to take your place for a time. And let Giles come along

too, by all means. We'll find room for him. I am taking
my young grandson and they can be companions on the
voyage.' For Lord Badger did not think that his grandchildren were too good to play with village-boys, as Sir
Anderson thought that his sons were.

But Giles said: 'It wouldn't be fair for me to go without
Bronwen. She would have nobody to play with.'

Bronwen laughed: 'Don't be silly, Giles. You aren't so
important to me as all that. I have plenty of girl friends.
And *I* wouldn't go to Africa even if I was invited. I don't
like lions or tigers at all; if one must have them I think
they are safer in cages.'

There is not much left of the story to tell. The treasure
was said to be worth about fifteen thousand pounds.
Bronwen and Giles talked over how this money should
be divided and they agreed that they should have one-
third each, and that Sergeant Harington should have the
remaining third. That meant that they would have four
thousand pounds each, most of which they would put in
the bank. Before Lord Badger went back in his car,
Bronwen's mother said that she and Bronwen and
Bronwen's uncle would willingly look after the Castle
for a few months while Sergeant Harington was away in
Africa. Sergeant Harington told Lord Badger that they
would be suitable people for the task, so Lord Badger
accepted their offer.

Then Giles and Sergeant Harington hurriedly bought
sun-helmets and hot-weather clothes for Africa and went
off in a big ship with Lord Badger. In Africa they saw
all the wild animals they wanted to see and took photo-
graphs of some of them and had a really good time, and
came back safely three months later.

They found that the Castle had been very well kept
in their absence by Bronwen and her mother. A wooden
staircase had now been built up the turret for visitors
who wished to see the treasure-room; and it had been a

very busy time, for two hundred thousand visitors had come to see it and Bronwen's uncle had to stand at the door all day saying, 'Pass along, please. There are other visitors waiting to come up.' The wooden staircase had been built right up to the top of the turret and the stream of visitors, when they had seen as much as Bronwen's uncle allowed them to see, went on to the top of the turret and then down by another wooden staircase to the path around the top of the walls where Sergeant Harington had tied the rope to the railing that evening. Everything in the chests had been put neatly into glass cases with explanations written by the antiquarians, and there was a strong electric lamp fixed to the ceiling so that people did not need to use pocket-torches. Giles and Bronwen's clay model of the Castle was put here too. People came from all over the world to see this famous room.

Sergeant Harington was Castle-keeper again and was paid twice as much money as before because so very many more tickets were now sold. He became quite rich and in the summer season sold six pounds' worth of postcards and guidebooks every day. Giles and Bronwen remained good friends, and are nearly grown up now. They both bought ponies and learned to hunt at the same time.

As for Sir Anderson Wigg, the story of his plot against Sergeant Harington got about – one of the antiquarians told it to the people at The Bull. The story made everyone very angry with Sir Anderson. The village men no longer touched their caps to him because they said that he was no gentleman; and the gentry no longer accepted his invitations to meals, because they said he was a bad sportsman. So he decided to sell Lambuck Hall again, and go back to London and his jam factory, and be more careful in future. Sergeant Harington was the buyer of the house, and bought it cheap and turned it into a hotel

called 'The Crown'. It became very well-known to travellers, for Bronwen's mother managed it excellently for him.

As for Mr Slark, he was fined five pounds for scattering waste-paper and considered himself lucky not to have been sent to prison instead. He remained faithful to Sir Anderson Wigg and drove his car for him for many years without a single accident.

Afterword

The manuscript of *An Ancient Castle* is now a half-century old and is something of a small treasure in itself. Like the jewels discovered in the hidden room in the story the forty-nine pages of typescript have lain stored away in archives until quite recently. The foolscap sheets of the story have been heavily reworked and corrected in Graves' handwriting but he apparently abandoned the work sometime in the early 1930s. It remained in this corrected but unfinished state among his papers and was included in a batch of his manuscripts offered for sale by the author. The material was bought in June 1975 by the London dealer in rare books Anthony Rota, who in turn offered *An Ancient Castle* to the University of Victoria in British Columbia. The Special Collection Librarian at the University, Howard Gerwing, realized that the manuscript would make an important addition to the University's already extensive Graves collection and he persuaded the University to buy it.

It was here that *An Ancient Castle* was brought to my attention by Christopher Petter while I was working on my textual critical edition of Graves' poetry. The text has been prepared from the original manuscript and incorporates the approximately 3,000 words of the author's handwritten corrections and also his revisions in punctuation.

In preparing the text for publication, a small number of minor inconsistencies in fact and style have been corrected. The fundamental objective has been to produce an edition that expresses the writer's intent of producing a children's story and not of delivering a strictly scholarly edition with an elaborate critical apparatus. This is not to say that *An Ancient Castle* has no value to the literary scholar, for the work echoes many of Graves' sentiments set out in his autobiography, *Good-Bye to All That*, first published in 1929. The adult reader of *An Ancient Castle* will recognize again the author's hatred of trench-warfare, his belief in a code of honour, sportsmanship and fair play, his disgust with the technology of destruction and his loathing of army jam. Some readers may construe *An Ancient Castle* as a parable and find a good many parallels with the autobiography, yet for all this it remains an exciting and entertaining children's story.

The manuscript deserves further study by literary scholars, particularly those interested in Graves' stylistic development, because the first two pages have a number of pencilled revisions in what appears to be Laura Riding's handwriting. These give some indication of the way in which Graves and Riding collaborated at that time. It should be noted, however, that in the preparation of this edition Laura Riding's corrections have been ignored and the text used is that of Graves only.

After abandoning *An Ancient Castle* Graves did not attempt another children's book, apart from a condensation of his *Lawrence and The Arabs* (1935), until *The Penny Fiddle* (1960), a collection of poems. He continued with *The Big Green Book* in 1962, *Ann at Highwood Hall* (1964), *Two Wise Children* (1966) and *The Poor Boy Who Followed His Star* (1968).

I would like to acknowledge the kindness and encouragement of Robert and Beryl Graves during the preparation of this edition and also the generosity and assistance of the staff in the Special Collections Division of the McPherson Library at the University of Victoria, especially Howard Gerwing and Christopher Petter. The task of preparing the work would have been impossible without the help of Elizabeth Saunders of the *Malahat Review* who typed several drafts of the text. The generosity of the Canada Council in making it possible for me to visit Robert Graves in 1974 in company with Robin Skelton, who made the introduction, must also be acknowledged.

Corpus Christi College   William David Thomas
Cambridge, 1980.